Alexander stepped in close to her and pushed his hands into the thick mass of her golden hair. His fingers bunched in it at the base of her neck, pulling her head back, exposing the creamy white skin of her throat and thrusting her breasts up at the same time. He lowered his lips down to the sensitive skin of her throat and took a taste of her—the flavor of her seemed to ignite a spark in his mind and body.

Novels by Leigh Savage

<u>Saint Louisville Vampire Series</u>
Angel of Death
Shadows of my Past

Stand Alone Novels
Bound by Blood: Short Story Collection
Dream Dragon the Dark Side of Poetry
Goldie's Three Bears

**Children Books written under the name
Carrie Lea Williams**

The Smile Box: A Story about Feelings
The Swan and the Rose: A Story about Inner Beauty

Thanks to all the Wicked Women and Wicked Seductions Publishing Company without them this project would never have come to be.

A Special Thanks to the lovely **Seraphina Donavan** for creating the cover art for this book.

You may find out more about Seraphina and her work here:

https://www.facebook.com/seraphina.donavan

https://www.facebook.com/pages/Seraphina-Donavan/211121168972963?fref=ts

http://www.amazon.com/Seraphina-Donavan/e/B008TCY3I6/ref=sr_tc_2_0?qid=1432400436&sr=8-2-ent

Zeus – Supreme God
Hera – Goddess of Marriage
Moerae – Goddess of Destiny
Eros - God of Love
Charon - Death

3 Sisters of Fate

Klotho - Spins the thread of life
Lachesis – Measures the threads of life with her staff
Atropos – Cuts the threads of life

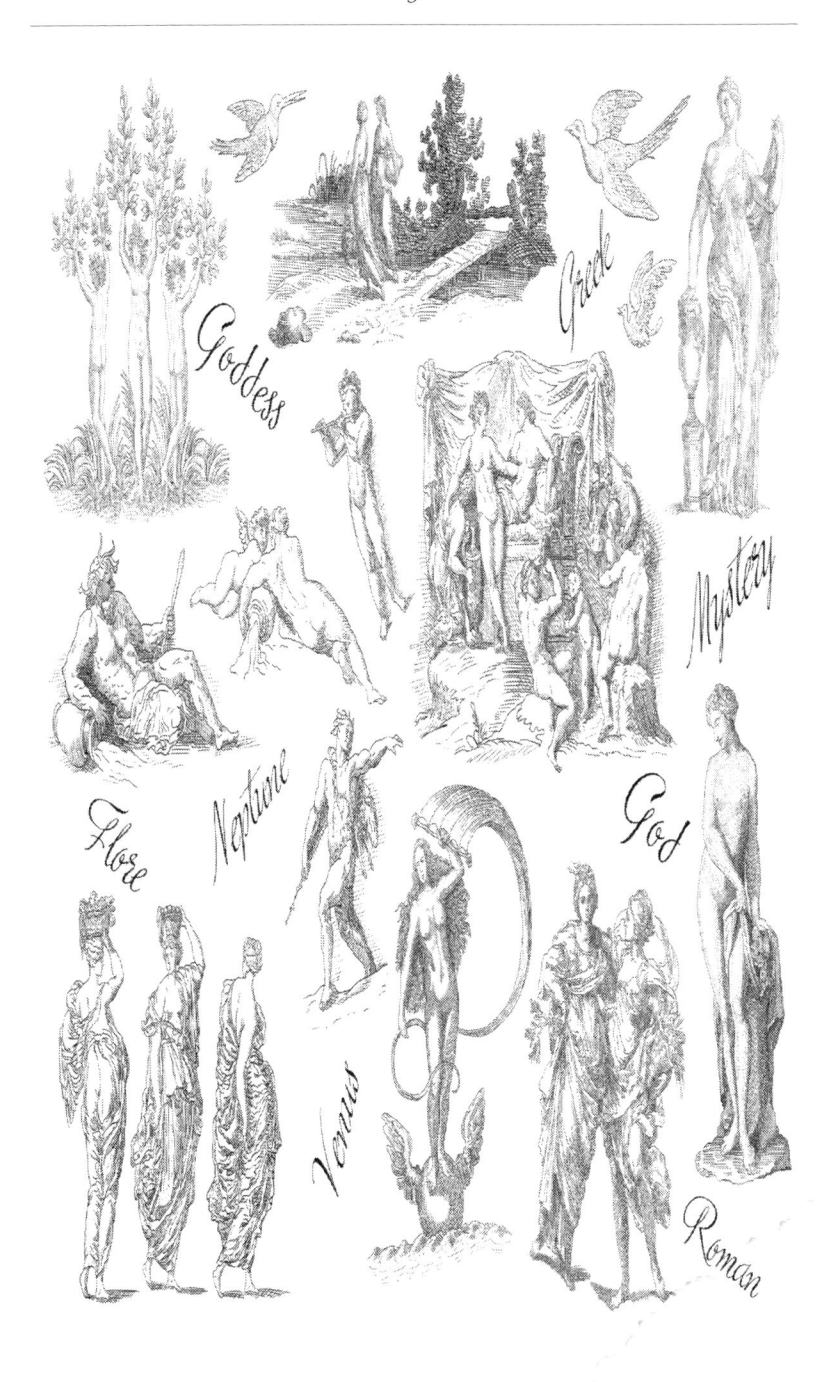

Goddess Greek Mystery Flore Neptune God Venus Roman

Twisted Destinies

By Leigh Savage

CHAPTER ONE

Chamber of the Fates

Moerae walked into the chambers, glancing over to where the Fates were working and unlike her, they seemed content doing their jobs.

Klotho sat there, dutifully spinning the threads of mortals' lives while tapping her foot.

Lachesis walked around with her staff, carefully measuring each mortal's allotted time on earth while humming softly.

Atropos used her abhorred sheers to cut the threads of the mortals' lives with a satisfied glint in her eyes.

The sisters didn't stop what they were doing to greet or even acknowledge her, as she walked across the room toward the pool she used to peer into the mortals' world.

She'd grown tired of her job, writing mortals' destinies and never getting to live her own life. If she were truthful with herself, she could admit she was feeling lonely. That's why she envied the Fates, because they had each other and she had no one. She needed to find something to entertain herself and give herself a break from this mundane job thrust upon her by Zeus, but even Zeus would take time off and visit the mortal world from time to time, so why couldn't she?

Moerae leaned over, peering into the crystal clear pool and waved her hand, skipping through a vast amount of mortals' lives, searching for something unique and worth her time.

She found exactly what she was looking for—the most stunning mortal she'd ever seen. He looked tall, muscular, with long thick black hair pulled back in a thong and the most stunning green eyes she'd ever seen. He reminded her of the old Greek statues the muses always seemed to inspire the artists to create.

Intrigued, she attempted to view his destiny but was unable to see anything about his future. It could only mean one thing…he must be a demigod.

Gods and demigods were the only ones she couldn't write or affect their destiny and the sisters couldn't decide their fate. Since the gods had no control over the demigods, Zeus decreed that it was forbidden to lay with a human, in fear of creating more demigods…knowing they would only bring chaos to the natural order.

It didn't matter to her, because he was exactly what she needed to spice up her life. She would just have to make sure the sisters didn't find out, or they would call upon Zeus and he would order his death before she even had a chance to have her fun with him.

Yes, it was time for a vacation.

CHAPTER TWO

Mortal Realm
Sixty Six Bar…Saint Louis, MO

Moerae viewed him from across the bar; he seemed even more striking in person. He wore a black suit that fit him like a second skin accompanied by a blue tie, matching the color of his eyes perfectly. He carried himself with all the arrogance of the gods he was descended from.

Women seemed to flock around him, throwing themselves at him but with one look into his emerald green eyes, she could sense he felt bored and uninterested in what was being offered to him so freely.

She seriously doubted he'd ever heard the word no…and it was probably about time she taught him the meaning of the word, along with a few other things she had in mind.

Walking further into the bar, she sat down across from where he stood, making sure she sat in plain view. After all, she wasn't just any woman, she was a Goddess and he would just have to come to her. If she got her way, she would have him bowing down to her, before she was done with him.

"What can I get for you miss?" the bartender asked.

"Strawberry Daiquiri."

~*~*~

Alexander sipped at his scotch while paying little interest to the women who were fawning over him…none of them were worth his time. He wanted a woman who was sexy, passionate and independent…different than the rest.

He glanced across the bar and that's when he saw her. She had pale blond hair, cascading down her creamy bare shoulders and her eyes were a hypnotic gold. *Yes, very different, all right.* The rest of her remained hidden from view by the bar; he needed to see more of her.

Getting up from the bar, he made his way over to the beautiful blonde lady. When he turned the corner, the rest of her came into view. She wore a sky blue dress that clung to every glorious curve of her body and came down to her knees. Her bare legs peeked out from the dress, giving him another glimpse of her creamy white skin. Something about the way she carried herself made him stir at the sight of her and he knew he must have her.

Taking the seat next to her, he waved over the bartender. "Scotch on the rocks…she's buying," Alexander stated while pointing to the blonde.

"Why would I be buying you a drink?" Moerae asked sharply.

"Because you're so hot…when I looked at you it caused the ice in my drink to melt, ruining perfectly good scotch, so it's only fair that you replace it."

Alexander saw the corners of her mouth lift in a slight smile and he knew he'd piqued her interest. He leaned in closer to her and whispered, "What's your name?"

"Moerae."

He loved the sexy tone she used and he smiled again. "I'm Alexander." He took her hand, pressing his lips to her palm. "It's a pleasure to meet you," he whispered softly against the palm of her hand.

Looking deeply into her golden eyes he swore he could see embers of desire spark. He fought the urge to run his fingers up along her arm and down her back, so he could feel the softness of her creamy white skin.

~*~*~

Moerae swore she could feel heat emitting from his body as he leaned in closer to her, gradually melting away her resolve to teach him the meaning of the word no. Then, when he took her palm into his hand and brought his lips down over her sensitive skin, it caused chills to run up the length of her arm. It awakened a need inside her that had long been denied. Nothing else seemed to matter, except for the need she was experiencing.

Moerae got up from the barstool, leaned in close to his ear and whispered, "Follow me."

Alexander threw some money down on the bar and quickly got up to follow her out.

She smirked; it seems he paid for both their drinks after all.

CHAPTER THREE

Chamber of the Fates

Eros paused at the chamber door where Moerae and the Sister Fates worked. He wasn't looking forward to delivering the message to Moerae.

He wondered how she would take the news of Zeus' command for them to wed. He didn't have a say in the matter and it was beyond him. He'd heard Moerae was beautiful but he never saw himself as a one woman type. He loved to love women and any time he was with one woman, she would become tired and be finished with their love making before he was even close to being done.

It didn't really matter what he wanted though, he must obey Zeus. Taking a deep breath, he entered the chamber. "I have a message for Moerae," Eros announced while glancing over to where the sisters were working. He couldn't help but to drink in the sight of their luscious, curvy bodies, barely covered by the see-through white dresses they each wore. He sensed himself growing hard at the sight of them and a rebellious thought flicked through his mind…why couldn't he have been commanded to wed the Fates instead?

Many of the immortals were scared of the sisters, because it was rumored they could even meddle with the Fates of the immortals if they chose to. Nobody knew for sure how much power they possessed.

Now, finally getting to lay eyes on the goddesses himself, he thought they were the most gorgeous females he'd ever seen.

So many of the goddesses had pale blonde hair but the three of them possessed hair like fire and looking at them seemed to be setting his blood on fire while their piercing blue eyes seemed like they could look right into your soul.

He wondered if the other rumor he'd heard was also true—did they really share their men? He couldn't help to imagine what it would be like to have all three of them crying out in pleasure while he took turns fucking each of them until they were completely spent.

Upon hearing his question, all three sisters stopped what they were doing and stared at him intently.

Eros could see the pink tips of their nipples through their white dresses and he wanted nothing more than to take them into his mouth. Then, he wondered if when they stood up, would he see red curls between their thighs as well?

He felt himself grow even harder at the mere thought and had to fight the urge to adjust his erection. Hell, he better be quick…deliver the message and leave…before he got himself into trouble, but then again, he wasn't married yet. He wanted to make each one of them beg for him to bring them release, and then take them all over again and again.

~*~*~

Klotho glanced up and recognized Eros by the mere sight of him. He'd always been the most handsome out of the gods and she couldn't help but to feel excitement coursing through her veins. She and her sisters were just discussing how they were in need of some entertainment since Moerae went on vacation. If the rumors were true about Eros' prowess as a lover…He would prove to be just what they needed.

Klotho rose and walked toward him and while she passed each of her sisters, they stood and joined her. They walked leisurely over to him, knowing he could see their large breasts and the red curls between their thighs.

Gazing into his eyes, she could see raw hunger. Glancing down, she could see the bulge between his legs and couldn't help that her tongue darted out to lick her lips in anticipation of what she imagined she and her sisters could do to him…with him….for him.

CHAPTER FOUR

Mortal Realm
Four Seasons Hotel St. Louis, MO

Alexander walked her to the door of her hotel room and told himself over and over again on the walk there, that he would take his time with her.

Then their lips touched and all good intentions fled his mind, her body leaned in to his seductively and he wanted nothing more than to take her right then and there. "If you're going to tempt me like this you may want to move this inside before I devour you right here on the spot for everyone to see," he whispered in a husky voice.

Moerae reached into her purse and pulled out the electronic key for the room, hurriedly swiping it and opening the door. She flicked on the lights while pulling him into the room with her at the same time, then swiftly shut the door.

Right there in the entrance, Alexander stepped in close to her and pushed his hands into the thick mass of her golden hair. His fingers bunched in it at the base of her neck, pulling her head back, exposing the creamy white skin of her throat and thrusting her breasts up at the same time. He lowered his lips down to the sensitive skin of her throat and took a taste of her—the flavor of her seemed to ignite a spark in his mind and body.

He drew in a deep breath to try to get some control back. Leaning over Moerae, his lips were just about to touch hers while their eyes stayed connected. "I love the taste of your skin. I can't wait to taste more while my tongue devours you."

In the next instant, Moerae stepped back then dropped the dress from her body in one swift fluid motion, letting it fall to the floor. She stood before him in nothing but her black high heels.

Alexander couldn't help but smile with a devilish grin upon realizing she hadn't been wearing any undergarments under her dress. The thought of it made him grow even harder, when he didn't think it possible to want her any more than he already did.

Now though, he knew she had a naughty streak in her and it made him want her even more. He grew tired of always finding women with no sense of adventure when it came to the bedroom. They all seemed to just go through the motions with no fire, no imagination. He wanted a woman who would equal him when it came to satisfying his desires and her own.

Pulling back while loving the way her kiss-swollen lips looked, he knew he wanted to kiss her elsewhere. Pushing her down onto the bed, he knelt down between her legs and buried his face into her soft blonde curls. He plunged his tongue deep within her, enjoying the sweet taste of her and the sounds of her moans while she writhed against his mouth in pleasure.

Alexander then took his fingers and pressed three into her while he continued to lick and suckle her clit.

~*~*~

Moerae watched him while he removed his clothing; his body, truly a work of art. At the site of his massive erection her breath caught. Just by looking at him she felt her juices dripping between her thighs.

Moerae now felt like she would go up in flames as his tongue went back and forth, licking and suckling her clit, then plunging into the core of her. Desire built inward, waiting for sweet release but not quite reaching it. Then his fingers stroked and dipped into her while his mouth continued assaulting her clit.

She pushed against the onslaught of his mouth and fingers. "Now," she cried out, not sure what she asked for. All she knew is how she wanted—no needed more. She wanted to feel him deep within her—now.

Rising up, Alexander positioned himself between her thighs. Lifting her slightly, he deliberately pressed deeply into her, gradually pulling back until just the tip of his cock remained inside her before reentering her again. He moved with an unhurried and languid pace, watching the expressions crossing her face while he slowly increased the speed of his thrusts.

Her fingers dug into his flesh while her legs wrapped around him as he continued to bury himself deeply. She cried out in release and he followed her over the edge.

CHAPTER FIVE

Chamber of the Fates

Klotho moved closer to where Eros stood, waiting for their response. She could sense his nervousness, but she could also sense some other emotion coming from him.

She couldn't help feeling excited while she walked towards him, letting her hips sway seductively. Feeling anxious and way too warm in her dress, she looked Eros over.

This god was well built, tall with blond hair hanging to his shoulders and the most alluring sky blue eyes.

It'd been eons since the last time she and her sisters shared in the comforts a man could bring.

Her sisters looked as intrigued as she felt while they joined her to stand before Eros.

Klotho stopped directly in front of him with Lachesis and Atropos on either side of her. She reached out, running her finger down along his chest, stopping just above the waistline of his jeans.

Her sisters, Lachesis and Atropos each latched onto one of his arms.

"Come now, Moerae isn't here right now and we rarely get visitors, join us while we wait for her return," Klotho suggested while pressing against him, letting him feel the soft curves of her body against his hard body.

"I guess there's no harm in visiting for a while," Eros responded.

"Follow me," Klotho prompted.

Just then, her sisters helped to lead him to their sleeping chambers. Lachesis and Atropos led Eros to the large bed in the center of their room. They released his arms, then they turned towards him and promptly let their white dresses fall to the floor.

Now, they stood naked before him.

Klotho stood in-between her two sisters, following suit as she also let her white dress join the other two dresses on the floor.

This was a clear and united invitation to the god who looked both stunned and eager while gazing at their bodies naked before him.

~*~*~

Eros felt his erection grow so hard he thought the pain would drive him mad. Just the seductive sight of the three sisters standing there at the end of the bed, made him hungry for the Fates to control his lust filled destiny.

He couldn't believe his eyes when they each removed their white dresses, exposing luscious breasts, curvy hips and those lovely red curls between their thighs, now completely bared for his viewing.

Hastily, he removed his garments which promptly joined the pile of dresses on the floor. He heard them gasp when he let his pants down, freeing his massive erection from the binding of his jeans. He smiled, knowing they were pleased by what they viewed.

In the next instant, he felt himself being pushed back onto the bed as the three of them joined him.

~*~*~

Klotho had always been the one with an oral fixation, so she immediately positioned herself between Eros' legs. While she did, she saw Lachesis straddling herself over Eros mouth, so she could get her pussy licked. Atropos sat back against the plush pillows watching her, one hand playing with her tits and the other hand toying with her clit.

Anxious, Klotho lowered her mouth over his erection, swirling her tongue around the head of his cock, and then she lowered back down until she could feel his balls against her lips. She could hear him grunt while she repeated the movements over and over, enjoying the taste of him in her mouth.

All the while, Eros moved his tongue in and out of Lachesis' pussy with extreme greediness and seeming skill.

Klotho watched him even as she sucked on him and the visual display while she enjoyed her oral play was torturing her. She couldn't take it anymore and she could feel her desire dripping down her legs—she needed to appease her wet snatch—to feel him inside her.

Rising up and positioning herself over his erection, she gradually lowered herself, guiding his cock inside her with her hand. He seemed so huge that it took a moment for her pussy to adjust to his massive size.

Gradually, deliberately, she began to rock against him in a way that caused her clit to rub against him while his cock slid within her slick, wet pussy. She loved the way he felt buried deep in the innermost part of her it; felt as if they'd become one. She couldn't remember a time when she felt this way about any male. Eros made her feel alive and she wondered if—hoped it was true about his appetites and his stamina, she and her sisters were very lonely and very hungry for some hot loving, and he may be just the god for them.

~*~*~

Eros growled low in his throat at the feel of his cock deep inside Klotho's dripping, wet pussy. He thought he would come immediately but instead, he tried to focus on Lachesis. To his own great pleasure, he continued to thrust his tongue into her, bringing her closer to her orgasm.

Reaching up, he gripped her by the hips and held her in place as he thrust his tongue more deeply into her sweet pussy. Still, he wasn't satisfied, taking one of his hands, he thrust three fingers deep while he continued to suck on her clit. Curling his fingers until he was able to find her special spot, he heard her cry out in release.

Eros didn't release Lachesis, instead he held her tightly in place as he continued his attentions, her pussy causing her to cry out over and over until at last, her body collapsed limply against him.

Eros allowed Lachesis to sluggishly move to the side. With delight in his heart at the glorious job she'd been doing of riding his cock hard, he took one of Klotho's large breasts into each of his hands. Taking her nipples between his fingers, he began to tug on them lightly, enjoying the soft sounds of pleasure she made while she accelerated her movements over his rigid cock.

Eros knew he was an immortal, but if he could die from pleasure this would be the time, these Sisters Fate were the perfect mates for him and his sexual drive. He could enjoy them in turn for hours. He grinned…hell he could enjoy this forever.

CHAPTER SIX

Mortal Realm
Four Seasons Hotel St. Louis, MO

After a few minutes, while they both panted to catch their breath, Moerae got up from the bed and retrieved Alexander's tie from the floor and returned to the bed where he lay. "Give me your hands," she commanded.

Alexander did as he was told, not realizing what she had in store, but completely willing to go along with whatever she wanted if it meant he could spend more time with her. This was the kind of wild, wanton woman he'd always longed for. She surprised him and he loved every second of it. He couldn't remember the last time he'd been with a woman so full of passion and it was refreshing to have someone who could be an equal in the bedroom.

Moerae straddled him and wrapped the tie around his wrists, binding them together.

"Wait, if you bind my hands together, I won't be able to touch you and I so want to touch you—all of you."

"Where would you like to touch me first?" Moerae asked seductively.

"I want to touch your breast," he responded.

"Like this?" she asked, while she cupped her own breast in her hand and gently tugged on her nipple with her fingers until her nipples were taut peaks.

"Yes," he responded in a rasping voice, as his cock stirred to life once more while he could feel her wetness on his abdomen.

"What would you like to do next?"

"I want to touch your wet pussy!"

Moerae traced her hand down her body until her fingertips touched her clit. "Like this?"

"No, I want to feel inside you!"

She dipped her fingers within herself. "Like that?" she asked in a gasp.

"Yes!" he replied with an anxious plea in his voice, "Now, let me taste you!"

Removing her fingers, she brought them to his lips.

He eagerly took her fingers into his mouth, sucking the wetness from her fingertips. *Yes!* This woman knew what would turn him on. "More please."

Moerae then moved so she hovered over his face, teasing him before she let him devour the juices from her pussy as she ground against his mouth. Her whole body was visibly trembling at the sensations his mouth was creating. She grabbed her breasts, squeezing them together, adding to the pressure building internally while she cried out in release.

"You taste amazing," he said as his breath was fanning over her sensitive pussy.

Moerae moved down, bringing her lips to his, tasting herself on his lips. "Now, it's time for me to taste you," she spoke against his lips. She moved down, positioning herself between his legs, taking his cock into her hands as she lowered her mouth over his massive erection. Swirling her tongue around the head of his cock, she then took him fully into her mouth. She heard him groan while her mouth moved up and down his shaft.

"Moerae," he cried out in a harsh whisper as he spilled his seed into her mouth.

Moerae felt the pulsing of his cock in her mouth just as he exploded; she didn't remove her mouth, instead she swallowed every last drop, enjoying the taste of him.

This vacation thing was a glorious experience and this demigod was so right for her, just as she thought he would be. She wanted to enjoy him for as long as possible.

CHAPTER SEVEN

Mortal Realm
Sixty Six bar…Saint Louis, MO

Moerae sat nervously at the bar, waiting for Alexander. They'd been spending the afternoons out on the town and spent the nights in each other's embrace. He'd only been gone for a couple of hours, but she already missed him and the way he made her feel when she was around him. It seemed crazy to feel this strongly for him in such a short time.

It wasn't supposed to be like this. She was a goddess and she knew better. She intended to just have fun, not getting involved and having feelings for the man. She quickly slammed down the rest of her drink in one swig. What was she going to do? Her time in the mortal world would be over soon. She would have to leave him and return to MOUNT OLYMPUS.

"CAN I BUY YOU A DRINK?" A MAN SLURRED AT HER WHILE HE LEANED IN CLOSE TO HER.

"NO THANKS, I'M WAITING FOR SOMEONE," MOERAE REPLIED, NOT PAYING MUCH ATTENTION TO THE DRUNKEN MAN.

"NO ONE'S HERE NOW," HE SAID AS HE REACHED OUT, TOUCHING HER ARM. "SO, DON'T BE A BITCH."

Moerae turned around. "Excuse me? I think you better remove your hand from my arm and leave," she said in a firm voice, getting a quick flash from the man's life and she didn't like what she saw; darkness surrounded this Gabriel and she didn't care to see any more than she had to. She wasn't here to work and didn't want to interfere with whatever destiny or fate that had already been written for him.

She couldn't help but notice how his breath and clothes reeked of alcohol. His brown hair looked unkempt and even his clothing looked like he'd slept in them.

"I see you're too good for someone like me," Gabriel responded rudely while he squeezed her arm.

"I said leave." Moerae raised her voice carefully to keep her emotions under control, she couldn't lose control and let the appearance of being a mortal disappear. Normally, she would use her powers and rid herself of this mortal but she couldn't risk being seen in her true form.

"Who do you think you are?" Gabriel hissed at her.

Moerae could feel the change coming over her and from experience, she knew her eyes would start to glow and they would quickly give her away. She fought to get her emotions under control before the mortals around her could notice.

Alexander entered the bar and at once, he headed to Moerae.

Everyone in the bar could see the man wasn't taking no for an answer as he quickened his pace, coming up behind the guy. "The lady said for you to leave." Alexander said from behind the man harassing Moerae.

UPON HEARING ALEXANDER'S VOICE, MOERAE FELT RELIEVED HE'D COME TO HER RESCUE AND IMMEDIATELY, HER EMOTIONS CAME BACK UNDER CONTROL.

ALEXANDER WAS TALLER AND MORE MUSCULAR THAN THE MAN WHO'D BEEN HARASSING HER, SO IT WASN'T ANY SURPRISE WHEN THE MAN BACKED DOWN QUICKLY AFTER ONE LOOK AT ALEXANDER.

AFTER MAKING SURE THE GUY LEFT THE BUILDING, HE CAME BACK TO STAND NEXT TO MOERAE. "ARE YOU ALL RIGHT?"

"YES, THANK YOU. IS IT OKAY IF WE LEAVE HERE?" SHE ASKED, FEELING SLIGHTLY SHAKEN OVER THE WHOLE ORDEAL. SHE JUST CAME SO CLOSE TO REVEALING HER TRUE SELF, AND THEN EVERYTHING WOULD HAVE BEEN OVER BEFORE SHE EVEN GOT TO SAY GOODBYE.

"That's fine," Alexander replied.

CHAPTER EIGHT

The Sisters of Fate Bedchambers

Lachesis loved the feel of his mouth on her pussy; then when he clutched her, holding her in place while he continued his oral assault, she thought she would die. Then, Eros thrust his fingers inside of her while sucking on her clit and in a matter of moments a glorious, warm orgasm washed over her entire body. Though he didn't stop there, he continued the onslaught against her pussy, causing her to cry out over and over until her whole body went limp.

Gingerly, Lachesis moved off of him, so she could lie down next to him, then she leaned over, kissing his lips that were covered in her pussy juices. Releasing his mouth, she ran her fingers over his muscular chest, placing her large breast into his face. She was rewarded when his warm mouth latched onto her nipple, causing desire to pool between her legs again, despite the fact that she'd had more orgasms in a row than she'd ever experienced before. She thought there was no way her body would again grow needy so soon after being thoroughly pleasured. Instantly, she used the tips of her fingers and dipped inward until she could feel her wetness as she imagined what it would feel like once she had him inside her.

She so hoped her sisters were enjoying him the same way, although by their cries and moans of pleasure, she felt sure they enjoyed this god as much as she did.

~*~*~

Eros enjoyed the muffled sounds of pleasure that Klotho made as he fondled her breasts but he was greedy and wicked and he wanted to hear her scream in pleasure. Grabbing her by the hips and holding her tight, he urged her to roll with him. Now, being on top, he saw that Atropos and Lachesis were laying there, masturbating while watching him with Klotho. It was the most erotic sight he'd ever seen.

He watched their movements intently as he thrust hard and deep into Klotho, pounding into her with a force that would hurt a mortal woman but by the sounds she was making, he knew she enjoyed each and every thrust.

Her constricting pussy tightened around his cock and he knew she edged close to her orgasm. He brought his head down, so he could suckle on her nipple as he continued to thrust inside her. Hearing her moans of ecstasy growing more insistent, he took her taut nipple between his teeth and tugged on it. He smiled smugly when she cried out in release.

Yes, I could live with this being my fate.

~*~*~

Atropos licked her lips as Eros moved toward her. His hand clutched hers, pulling it up; he took the fingers that had been within her and licked them clean.

"You taste so good," he purred with a wicked smile, "I want to drink you in." His breath fanned over the sensitive flesh of her pussy as he brought his lips down and leisurely dipped his tongue inside her.

Atropos cried out as the sensation of his tongue touched the innermost part of her body. Reaching down, she ran her fingers in his hair; holding him to her as she thrashed against his mouth. "More," she cried, desperate to be brought to release.

Abruptly pulling away, Eros seized her hips and sank himself within her. His balls slapping against her pussy as he repeatedly thrust into her. She met each thrust eagerly and she could feel herself drawing ever closer to the edge.

Atropos reached out, grasping an ass cheek in each hand and her nails dug into his flesh as she held him to her.

Eros pulled out of Atropos for a moment; gripping her by the ass, he used his hands to guide her, so she rolled over with her ass in the air. He slapped each ass cheek hard and his satisfaction increased when she cried out with a helpless pleasure. Feeling empowered, he plunged himself deep, pounding into her with all his force.

Her silken snatch pulsated against his cock and knew she was close. He reached around her body so his fingers could tug on her clit. Almost instantly, her body shuddered and then she whimpered helplessly in release, falling limp against the bed.

Eros reluctantly pulled out of Atropos and turned towards Lachesis, who continued to masturbate the whole time he'd been fucking Atropos. Lachesis being the only sister he hadn't gotten to be inside of yet and he imagined she would feel just as warm, slick and wet as the other two.

He'd also already given Lachesis the pleasure of an orgasm. He grinned wickedly. This time he would make her work for it.

Eros lifted each of Lachesis thighs and placed them on his shoulders as he positioned himself between her legs. Then he plunged into her completely until he could feel the wetness of her pussy against his balls. He could feel the wet folds of her pussy throbbing around his cock; he stopped while holding himself utterly still in her…at the same time, using his body weight skillfully to keep her from moving.

"Please; don't stop," Lachesis pleaded.

Upon hearing her pleas, Eros moved little by little, letting the pressure build anew until once again, her pussy pulsated around his cock. Then with a wicked deliberation, he once more held himself completely still.

"Eros," Lachesis cried out in a whimpering voice.

Eros smiled at her pleading and pounded into her even harder than before. This time however, when her sweet pussy vibrated around his cock he didn't stop. With a determined lust, he kept thrusting harder and deeper until he felt the sweet warmth of her orgasm cover his cock and heard the cries of her climaxing.

Feeling supreme, he thrust once more as his seed spilled into her. Pulling out of her, he noticed he still remained fully erect and this was exactly why one woman would never be enough for him, but three might be just right.

"Who's next?" Eros asked, smiling wickedly as he turned towards Atropos and Klotho.

CHAPTER NINE

Mortal Realm
Four Seasons Hotel...St. Louis, MO

"That's fine," Alexander said, as he followed her to the hotel. He was looking forward to having Moerae all to himself. He still couldn't believe how much he'd been affected by the sight of the other man touching his Moerae. Jealousy was something he'd never experienced before now. Then, he realized what he just thought to himself—he'd referred to her as his. More than anything, he found he wanted to lay claim to her heart, body and soul until she wanted him and only him.

Neither of them talked about what this relationship could be and he had no idea if she felt any real feelings for him or if she was just having fun, but one thing was for sure, he was falling for her and falling hard.

Alexander followed Moerae into the elevator of the hotel. He couldn't seem to push the image of the other guy's hands on Moerae out of his mind. He found he couldn't wait any longer though, he needed to have her right then and there. Pushing the emergency stop button after the door closed behind them, he intended to do just that. He wanted nothing more than to lay claim to her and make her all his.

Alexander drunk in the sight of Moerae as she turned toward him, her lips slightly parted as if she waited for him to kiss her.

She leaned slightly against the wall of the elevator and held onto the bar.

In a couple of quick strides, he closed the gap between them. "You're so beautiful that I can't wait another minute to touch you," he said in a rough voice while he pressed his hard body against her soft curves, he then brought his lips down on hers.

Moerae wrapped her arms around his neck as she pressed her body more fully against his while she deepened the kiss.

Breaking the kiss, he knelt down in front of her and ran his hands under her dress. Swiftly, he pulled down her black silk panties and tucked them into his pocket. Then, he pulled the dress up around her hips, so he could view the blonde curls between her thighs. "I have to taste your sweetness. You're like a drug that I can never get enough of," he purred as he gently took one of her legs, threw it over his shoulder and brought his lips to her pussy.

Moerae cried out when his tongue thrust into her. She reached out, lacing her fingers through his dark hair, holding on for dear life as she arched against the onslaught of his mouth.

Alexander responded to her cries by thrusting his fingers deep into her, loving the way her slick folds felt against his fingertips and the moans of pleasure he drew from her. With his fingers still in her, he took the bud of her clit into his mouth to suckle and nibble on the tender mound of flesh—and was rewarded with more cries of pleasure.

He stood up, withdrawing his fingers from the core of her desire and heard her cry of protest. He brought his fingers up to her parted lips and she took them into her warm moist mouth and sucked the pussy juices from his fingertips without being asked, as if she knew exactly what he wanted. "You're driving me mad," he groaned.

~*~*~

Moerae couldn't take anymore. Hurriedly, she undid his pants, letting them fall to the floor; releasing his raging head-on. Then kneeling down in front of him, she took the fullness of his cock into her mouth until her lips touched his balls while her hands gently massaged his balls in motion with her mouth.

She gazed up at him through veiled lashes as she continued sucking his cock while loving the expressions crossing his handsome face. It made her feel powerful in ways she'd never experienced before. That was saying something, considering she held power over every mortal's destiny. Until him and because of what he was, she couldn't control his destiny. For once in her existence, she liked the feeling of not knowing what would happen next.

Without warning, she suddenly felt desperate, knowing their time together would be short and she didn't want to waste time they didn't have. She released his cock as she stood up and brought her lips to his, kissing him as if indeed, this might be the last time.

His warm hands cupped her ass cheeks as he raised her up and lowered her down, entering her, pinning her back against the wall. She wrapped her arms and legs around him, bracing herself as he thrust deeply into her. Instantly, she flew over the edge, as he filled her completely. Her fingernails dug into his flesh as she bit down on her lips, muffling her cries of release.

She could feel him thrust deeply into her once more while he came inside of her as he groaned in his own release.

~*~*~

Alexander could feel her pulsating around his cock, then with one final thrust, he followed her over the edge. Slowly, he lowered her back down; holding her for a moment, so she could regain her footing before releasing her.

"I don't think I can ever get enough of you," Alexander whispered into her ear as he nibbled the sensitive flesh there, knowing it would cause goose bumps to travel down her arm and rekindle the flames between them. He loved the fact that he knew her body and how she would respond to him as if she'd been made just for him.

Feeling exhilarated, he bent down to pull his pants back up and moved over, releasing the emergency stop button, so he could have her again, in the privacy of the room. He gently patted his pocket that held her black panties and grinned, as he wasn't quite ready to return them to her just yet.

CHAPTER TEN

Mortal Realm
Sixty Six bar...Saint Louis, MO

Moerae waited at the bar for Alexander to return. He'd gone to his place to wash up and get another change of clothes. He'd asked her to come along, but she'd told him she would wait at the bar like she'd been doing. Once they'd made sure that man, Gabriel, from last time wasn't there.

Now, however she wished she would have gone to his place and seen where he lived. Though, she'd already been scared to find herself having feelings for him, and learning more about him would only make those feelings deepen. She couldn't let this happen. After all, there could be no happy ending for them.

Her time in the mortal world was almost over. She just received a message from Zeus summoning her to return and there was no way for her to take him with her…it wasn't allowed. No matter what happened so far, it seemed she was doomed to end up with a broken heart.

Moerae slammed the rest of her drink down, hoping it would make the uneasy feeling she'd been having all evening go away. She didn't understand how she knew something bad was about to happen, yet when she tried to look into the future it all became muddled and she couldn't make out anything. She'd been away from Olympus too long, so her powers were growing weaker or maybe—her emotions were affecting her powers.

It was so unlike her to be so conflicted about her emotions. She'd gone into this with one purpose and one purpose only…to have fun. She'd been having that fun but now, it was coming to an end and she didn't want it to be over.

After all, Alexander is a demigod and she couldn't see his destiny, much less try to change anything. Whatever is to be—would simply come to be and there was nothing she could do about any of it.

Moerae decided what she really needed to be worrying about was tonight. She planned to get up the courage to tell him this would be their last night together. She wished so badly to have more time with him but being summoned back now, she didn't have much choice. She would have to return sooner than planned and simply make the best of what little time they did have left.

Moerae wasn't the type to fool herself into thinking she would be able to return and see him again. No, she was a realist, being one of the fates made her one and she knew once she left, she wouldn't be returning to the mortal world during his life time.

CHAPTER ELEVEN

Alexander held the door leading to the alley open for Moerae as they exited the bar into the night air. Letting the door close behind them, he turned while noticing how the moonlight shone on Moerae's hair. She almost seemed like she didn't belong in this world. She seemed so perfect, so unique that he could easily believe she was an angel from heaven.

Alexander couldn't help himself yet again, he needed to kiss her right then and there. All day, he'd been fighting the feeling that something bad was about to happen, but he knew he couldn't stop whatever it might be. He really didn't understand the sense of premonition or the feeling of dread. However, his feelings of desire and need for her, he did understand.

Reaching out, he snatched her by the arm and spun her around to face him. "Moerae, you're absolutely breathtaking." He sighed against her lips before crushing his mouth to hers. He became utterly lost in the kiss.

Even through the headiness if their kiss, Alexander could swear he heard a sound coming from behind Moerae, glancing up, he saw a flash of silver coming towards her. Swiftly, he pushed her out of the way, placing his own body in front of her to shield her from what turned out to be a knife as it sank into his flesh.

Alexander gripped the man, struggling with him.

The man they met before looked enraged. "I'm done being the guy overlooked and ignored!"

Despite the throbbing pain that radiated from where the knife buried in his chest, Alexander's only concern was making sure he kept Moerae safe. He was able to free one of his arms from the struggle and he pulled his fist back, throwing a punch, knocking the man down.

"No!" the man shouted as he stumbled to the ground. "I thought I had a chance with her, but she's just like all the others!"

While the man ranted, it gave Alexander just enough time to pull the knife from his chest and as the guy lunged at him, the knife sunk into the other man's stomach.

The attacker went down to the ground and didn't get back up.

Alexander stumbled back toward Moerae, wincing in pain, only to fall down before he reached her.

"Are you all right?" she asked as she closed the distance between them and knelt down to where he lay. She started running her hands over his body, looking for the injury.

"I'll be all right," he lied, trying to keep his tone light; he knew the knife hit too close to his heart, there was a very good chance he wasn't going to make it, and help wouldn't make it to him in time. He didn't want to spend his last moments with her in an ambulance. No, he wanted to be next to Moerae to feel the warmth of her body and to know she was safe. It would be just fine to die if he did while looking at her lovely face.

~*~*~

Moerae's hand stopped over his chest when her fingers touched the warm sticky blood, covering his shirt. She pressed her hand firmly against his chest, trying to stop the gushing blood that seemed to be flowing way too freely. "HELP!" she cried out as tears fell down her cheeks.

"There is no help for him," Charon said as he emerged from the darkness of the alley.

Moerae peered up toward the voice and saw him then, emerging from the dark shadows. Death's Reaper. He wore a black suit, which she knew was made from a special material from the underworld to keep him hidden from the mortal's view.

His appearance always felt more than disturbing as compared to others in his station. His hair looked stark white and his eyes were a piercing icy blue.

"No you can't be here. Go away!" she screamed.

"It's not I who decides whose time has come and you more than anyone, know this to be true," Charon replied.

Alexander must have heard her talking as he asked, "Who are you talking too?"

"Don't worry Alexander. I won't let him have you." Moerae replied defiantly.

"Let who have me?"

"The Reaper!"

Alexander looked confused and he shook his head. "Moerae, whatever happens it's going to be all right because you're safe and that's all that matters, because without you— I wouldn't want to go on living."

"I love you Alexander—I can't lose you not now, when I just found you." Moerae sobbed as her eyes and skin begin to glow in the unearthly shimmer of the immortals as she lost control of her emotions, unable to hold onto her mortal appearance any longer.

The irony of the situation hit her full force, he wanted to protect her…When she was immortal…The knife would have done nothing to her but now, he was dying because he wanted to save her. She completely let go of her mortal illusion and embraced her Goddess form in preparation for the battle to come with the Reaper. "Leave us." Moerae commanded.

"You know I cannot leave without his soul," Charon replied as he stepped toward her.

At that moment, Moerae heard a gurgling sound coming from the ground a short distance away. She got up and walked over to the man who attacked them. Staring down, she saw that it was Gabriel. If only she'd taken a moment to pay attention to the darkness she'd felt coming from him, she could have rewritten his destiny and none of this would have ever happened.

Guilt washed over her; it was just as much her fault as this Gabriel's and it was up to her to find a way to fix it. Looking down at Gabriel, she noticed that he was still breathing while gasping for air. Anger made her push aside her guilt and she suddenly felt no sympathy at all for him. "Here, take his soul."

"It is not his time," Charon replied.

Moerae reached down. Her hand went through the man's chest as she ripped out the man's soul and flung it at Charon. "Now, it's his time. Take his soul and leave."

"I will collect this man's soul and take it to the underworld as a favor for you, but I will have to return and collect Alexander's soul, so I suggest you take this extra time to say your good-byes," Charon warned as he faded into the darkness with the Gabriel's soul in tow.

Moerae returned to where Alexander lay, kneeling down to grab both his hands in hers. She needed to hurry, for he was starting to awaken. Intending to take him out of the mortal plain, so the Reaper wouldn't be able to sense him and they could have more time together. Hopefully, this abrupt move would give her the time she needed to figure out a way to ultimately save his soul.

CHAPTER TWELVE

Goddess of Destinies Bedchambers

Alexander's memory seemed hazy as he started to come to and found himself in a strange place. He lay in a large round, plush bed, in the middle of a large golden hued room.

Turning slightly, he noticed Moerae lying next to him, watching him intently. "Where are we?" he asked, while he slowly became aware that Moerae wore a see through white dress, draped over her body in a very enticing way, making him completely forget any other questions in his mind.

Instead of answering, she leaned over to him, her lips only a breath away from his. "We are at my home," she replied as she brought her mouth down on his, pressing her body firmly against his.

Alexander felt the soft curves of her body molding to his and any thoughts of how they got here fled his mind. He became completely consumed with the feel of her supple flesh and her sweet lips as he deepened the kiss.

After a few minutes of wild, passionate kissing, he moved his lips away from hers. "Moerae, I have never wanted anyone as much as I want you. I just can't seem to ever get enough of you," he whispered against the hollow of her throat as his fingers trailed down, moving her white dress aside to expose one of her large, creamy white breasts.

Alexander heard the sharp intake of breath as he took one taut nipple into the warmth of his mouth and sucked on it while his other hand trailed down her body until his fingers felt the hem of her dress. Curling his fingers up, he pulled the dress higher, his hand moving underneath to find the core of her desire. Wetness met his fingertips as he gradually dipped his fingers into her.

"I love the way your body responds to my touch." He then switched to the other breast and moved his fingers ever so slowly inside her, enjoying the way she seemed to clinch around his fingertips and he knew she would feel the same way once he plunged his cock inside her and he couldn't wait to be deep into her warmth. He wanted to take things slow and enjoy every moment he spent with her. He didn't understand why but he somehow, he knew this could be their last time together and if it was…he wanted to make it last.

Moerae threaded her fingers through his hair, clutching him to her breast as she moved her hips, meeting the movement of his fingers. "I need you."

"Not yet," Alexander whispered against the skin of her sensitive nipple.

~*~*~

Moerae experienced such a deep disappointment when he withdrew his fingers from within her, but then she felt him clutch her by the hips as he silently directed her to roll over for him.

Lying on her stomach, he sprawled on top of her and she could feel his erection pressed against her ass, then he slid down her body as he trailed kisses along her spine. Nibbling on her ass cheeks and causing goose bumps to cover her flesh. Then, she could feel his fingers slowly slide back into her slickened folds. After a few moments, he added two more fingers, driving her to the edge and she cried out while she came.

Alexander withdrew his fingers and brought them to his lips. "You taste so sweet." His voice sounded low and rough with desire as he licked his fingers clean. Then he grabbed her hips, pulling her up slightly as he sunk into her gradually, then withdrew until just the tip of his cock remained inside her.

Then abruptly, he plunged fully into her, repeating the movement again and again until she came to yet another orgasm.

Thrusting once more, he followed her over the edge.

She could only lay there spent while he remained inside her, simply enjoying the feel of being filled by him and the warmth of his body pressed against hers.

Reaching around her body, Alexander grasped her breasts, cupping them in his hands as he continued to lie on top of her.

CHAPTER THIRTEEN

Mount Olympus, Throne of Zeus

"Charon, what brings you before my throne?" Zeus asked in a commanding voice from his throne.

"Zeus, I'm sorry, but it's Moerae. She has stolen a mortal's soul away that I was supposed to collect and has taken it out of the mortal realm to yours. I need your permission to collect the soul," Charon answered nervously as he gazed upon Zeus.

This god of all was quite intimidating to look upon even though he knew he wasn't the one in the wrong. Perhaps, it was the sheer size of him. Even with him sitting, he seemed larger than life and his voice filled the room. Very few would ever dare to cross Zeus and the few who had, paid the price for it.

"Sibylla! Thecla!" Zeus called out so loud the chamber rumbled.

"Yes, my lord." Sibylla and Thecla responded as the twin sisters ran towards the throne. Their long light brown hair cascading down their shoulders, nearly touching the floor as they knelt obediently before Zeus's throne.

"Sibylla, fetch Moerae and the mortal she's been consorting with and bring them before me immediately," Zeus commanded.

"Right away, my lord!" Sibylla replied as she ran toward the door, exiting the chamber to do his bidding.

"Thecla, fetch Atropos and Eros, then bring them here at once," Zeus ordered.

"Right away, my lord," Thecla responded as she exited the chamber just seconds after her sister.

~*~*~

Moerae awoke to the sound of pounding on her chamber doors. Quickly, she got up, walking over to the door to see who would dare disturb her. "Who's there?"

"It's Sibylla."

Moerae felt a sense of panic. Sibylla was one of Zeus' personal servants and if he sent her—it meant he knew. "Yes," she replied in a shaky voice.

"Zeus demands that you and your mortal appear before him at once," Sibylla ordered through the door.

Moerae had no choice except to appear before him and plead her case. Zeus wasn't known to be the most understanding of the gods and he would not take her disobedience of the rules lightly. Glancing over to where Alexander still slept peacefully, she knew that no matter what happened it'd been worth it just for the extra time she'd gotten to spend with him.

"Tell him we'll be right there," Moerae finally answered, and then made her way to the bed to wake Alexander and try to find the words to explain to him the truth about who she really was and where they actually were. She could only hope he wouldn't think she'd gone completely insane.

~*~*~

Zeus looked over the group he'd assembled before him, trying to decide where to start. The whole lot of them looked guilty.

Charon stood off to the side, waiting for Moerae and her mortal to enter the chamber.

Eros stood next to the Fates, even though he'd only asked for Atropos and he had no idea why the other two sisters tagged along.

"Eros, what were you still doing with the Fates? I sent you to deliver a message to Moerae, not to fool around."

"Zeus, my lord I respect that, but I simply cannot marry Moerae like you've ordered," Eros spoke firmly, trying to sound in charge of his own fate. He most likely knew Zeus still commanded him and he would be would be left with no choice but to obey. "I'm in love with the Fates."

Zeus stared at them with piercing eyes, seeing the truth…the Sister Fates were in love with Eros as well and despite the fact he was the one in charge, he didn't want to anger the Fates any more than any of the other Gods.

Just as Zeus was about to respond, Moerae entered the chamber with her mortal following behind her. He decided this Eros matter could wait and turned his attention to Moerae along with the confused looking mortal.

Moerae stared hard at Charon standing to the side of Zeus. Taking a deep breath, she gathered her courage for the battle ahead of her.

"Charon is this…" Zeus pointed to the mortal standing beside Moerae. "…The mortal whose soul you need to collect?"

"Yes," Charon responded.

"Atropos, make it so Charon can collect his soul," Zeus commanded.

"NO!" Moerae cried out, placing herself in front of Alexander.

"Moerae...I will deal with you later, for now, I have to set things right. Your actions have messed with the natural order and you out of anyone should understand the consequences you have set in motion."

Atropos stepped forward and glance at Moerae. "Sorry," she muttered as she took out her sheers and she took the mortal's thread in the other hand—about to cut.

"Please don't Atropos? I love him!" Moerae pleaded as she squeezed Alexander's hand.

"Zeus is right, it has to be set right," Atropos replied.

"It's all right Moerae, at least we got to be together one last time," Alexander stated firmly as if he understood everything now. He kissed her tenderly on the lips and turned to accept his final fate.

Atropos closed the sheers on the thread of his life and to her surprise—nothing happened. She gaped at Zeus in pure shock. "I'm sorry but I—I can't cut the thread."

"Impossible!" Zeus bellowed as he arose from his throne and walked over to the mortal. He reached into the mortal's chest and pulled his hand out, expecting to see the mortal's soul, instead his hand remained empty.

"STOP!" Klotho cried out, "Look! He's no longer mortal."

CHAPTER FOURTEEN

"How is this possible?" Zeus asked.

"He wasn't a normal mortal, was he Moerae?" Klotho asked.

Moerae gazed over at Zeus hesitantly before responding, knowing she would yet be in more trouble for not bringing the knowledge to Zeus attention the moment she discovered him. "No, he's a demigod."

"Charon, how exactly did he die?" Klotho asked.

"He was stabbed in the chest."

"And was he the intended target?" Klotho asked.

"No, I was," Moerae responded. "He was trying to save me." Moerae took Alexander's hand in hers and squeezed it, silently expressing her gratitude to him.

"It's only happened a couple of times in history, but a demigod can become a god if they sacrifice their life for another's," Klotho explained. "That was one of the reasons that we decreed gods should no longer reproduce with the mortals, as demigods mess with the natural order."

"Are you saying what I think you're saying?" Moerae asked, hoping more than anything what she was hearing was true.

"Yes, your mortal is now one of us." Klotho nodded.

"Can someone please tell me what's going on?" Alexander asked.

"You're a god now and that means you can stay with me forever," Moerae answered.

"Wait just a moment. Does that mean I don't have to wed Moerae?" Eros asked.

"What is this about me marrying Eros?" Moerae asked as she stared down Zeus.

All present had forgotten or were unaware that Moerae never received the message of their upcoming marriage ordered by Zeus.

"That was my idea," Hera spoke as she entered the room. Her golden brown hair arranged partly atop her head around the golden crown with several strands hanging down, her soft brown eyes were filled with excitement as she took up the spot next to her husband.

Hera looked every bit the part of the Queen of Goddesses. She stood with a regal air in her white satin dress, laced with silken threads while a gold chain hung around her neck, draping down her shapely body, adding to the rare beauty Hera was known for.

After all, it'd been Hera's beauty that attracted Zeus from the first moment he laid eyes on her and claimed her as his, right then and there.

"Why?" Moerae and Eros asked in unison.

"I was bored. With Aphrodite on vacation, I haven't had any marriages to plan, so I decided I would play match maker for once and Eros, I thought it was about time you find love. You were always the lover but never in love."

"I don't understand," Eros stated.

"I knew Moerae wouldn't be at the palace when you went to deliver the message of your upcoming marriage. However, I knew that you would be placed before the Goddesses of Fate and you wouldn't be able to resist the temptation of being with the three of them and that once you were with them…a perfect match would be made," she paused and gave Eros a wicked wink.

Eros looked stunned but he grinned widely and looked over at the Fate sisters with an expression of love on his face.

Hera nodded her head knowingly. "The Goddesses of Fate needed a god who had the stamina to satisfy all of their needs and you Eros…you would never be happy with one Goddess. However, being with three that's another story, now isn't it?" Hera asked, already knowing the answer.

"Yes, between them all, they have everything I ever wanted but could never find in one woman," he replied.

Hera paused and gazed over at her husband in askance.

He grinned broadly and slowly nodded his head.

Looking relieved and joyful, Hera she spoke loudly in the hall of gods, "So, there's only one thing left to do!"

"What's that?" Everyone asked at once.

"It's time to throw a double wedding!" Hera exclaimed as she clapped her hands with glee.

CHAPTER FIFTEEN

Hera gazed sweetly at Moerae, Lachesis, Atropos and Klotho as she walked up to each one, placing their wedding veils over their heads. The veils were golden vines that wrapped around with a sheer white material that flowed down their backs. She couldn't help admiring her handy work.

She glanced to Moerae. Her flowing white dress was sleeveless with golden accents through the sheer material and she wore golden sandals.

Lachesis also wore a white dress draped over one shoulder with a light silken material flowing behind her. The skirt of the dress split up along the leg, exposing the creamy white skin of her leg. Her waistline was adorned with silver beads that matched her silver sandals.

Atropos' pearl colored dress draped over both shoulders with pearl bead accents. The skirt embodied layers of transparent material that flowed down to her feet to hide the white sandals she wore.

Klotho dress dipped down low, exposing her creamy white cleavage with a high waistline, accented with rubies. The skirt hugged every curve and slightly flared out, hiding the red sandals she wore.

They were each radiating a rare beauty brought out by the love they held in their hearts.

Hera truly loved her job of being the Goddess of Weddings and she was particularly proud of this wedding. Not even Aphrodite herself could have done a better job playing match maker. Well, if she were truthful Aphrodite did help just a little, but still, she herself put the elaborate plan in motion and it worked out wonderfully.

"It's time ladies," Hera announced as she guided them to where they would walk out through the grand ballroom decorated for the feistiest of wedding celebrations.

~*~*~

Alexander glanced over at Eros, who also appeared to be nervous as they stood there waiting for the wedding to start. He still didn't quite understand how he ended up in this world he never even knew existed, but all that mattered to him is it meant he would get to be with Moerae forever.

He'd always known he was different, always wondered why all the women he'd met were so dull and boring. He knew of his striking looks and the magnetic pull he had with people. However, he never guessed it was because he came from the gods. He now knew why his mother never spoke of his dad. It all made sense, despite being surreal, along with the fact of how he supposed to live forever now.

That is fine with me as long as Moerae is by my side. Excitement rippled through him, as everyone went completely still and silent as the harp started playing and the goddesses came into view, each one was a vision but Alexander had eyes for only one and she was breathtaking.

CHAPTER SIXTEEN

Eros was all nerves as he waited next to Alexander. He couldn't believe his heart's desire was about to be realized. He kept worrying something would happen and it would not come to be. Maybe they would change their mind about sharing a husband.

Then, he heard the music. He looked up and saw the goddesses walking unhurried toward him and any uneasiness he felt vanished. The realization that he was about to marry three of the most beautiful goddesses who ever walked in Olympus hit him just now, and he couldn't be happier.

Later in the day, Eros sat with Lachesis to his right and Atropos at his left while Klotho sat on his lap. They all enjoyed the feel of the hot spring. They'd already made passionate love in their room before leaving to the hot springs but now, sitting in the hot soothing water he felt his cock becoming erect once more as Klotho's round ass brushed against his lap.

He glanced at Lachesis and Atropos, noticing that their breasts were bobbing in the heated water. Eros moved Klotho, so his cock slid into her slick folds and immediately, she started grinding against him while her breasts pressed against his chest.

Eros took one of his hands and let it travel in-between Lachesis' legs to find her bud. He did the same with his other hand to Atropos, causing both of them to struggle and moan in pleasure against the onslaught of his fingers as Klotho continued to fuck him until she cried out in release.

Eros watched as Klotho switched places with Lachesis.

Lachesis quickly straddled him and guided his cock into her wet pussy. She moved more fervently against him, pressing her breasts into his face. Eros took one breast with his mouth and sucked hard on her nipple, causing her to come instantly.

Eros watched as this time, Lachesis switched places with Atropos. Seizing Atropos by the hips, he guided her down over his cock as he helped her move against him and she eagerly sought her release. He could feel her tightening around his cock and knew she was close. He eagerly clenched an ass cheek in each hand, then squeezed. He smiled wickedly when he heard her whimpering in pleasure as she came as well.

Atropos rose up and knelt between Eros' legs, then wrapped her hands around his large hard cock. Lachesis and Atropos also knelt down on either side of her.

When Eros rose up out of the water, Atropos wasted no time taking Eros' erection into her mouth, sucking on him, then removing her mouth to allow each of her sisters to do the same and then back to her. They continued to take turns sucking his cock.

Soon, Eros felt that he was close to his own climax, so taking his cock in his hand he helped stroke while the three of them took turns sucking him to his breaking point.

All three women pulled away to kneel in front of him.

In the next instant, Eros's cum sprayed out, shooting Atropos, Lachesis and Klotho in the face.

Content now, he dropped back down into the water as Atropos, Lachesis and Klotho cuddled up next to him with audible sighs of satisfaction.

This must be the best dream a god could ever have. He planned to be good to all three of his lovely brides...*very* good.

CHAPTER SEVENTEEN

The night went by in a blur as they were whisked off to the Greek island of Samos…the same location Zeus and Hera had gone to for their honeymoon.

Moerae looked out through the glass door and watched the ocean waves. Opening the door, she stepped out onto the balcony, so she could hear the waves crashing against the shore when she heard Alexander walking across the room toward her, then she sensed the warmth of his body as he came up next to her.

"Did I tell you how beautiful you looked today?" he asked as he brushed her blonde hair aside, so he could kiss her bare shoulder.

"Yes," Moerae replied, "But I don't mind hearing it again." She leaned into his arms, enjoying the feel of his strength.

With a flick of his finger, the thin piece of material she wore fell to the balcony floor, bearing her naked body for his viewing. "But I think you look even more beautiful like this," he purred in a husky voice.

"Do you now," Moerae teased as she turned around, seeing he was shirtless but still wore his dress slacks. The breeze caressed her skin causing her nipples to tighten. She pressed her large breasts against his bare chest.

"How did I ever get so lucky?" Alexander asked.

"You have the luck of the gods," Moerae whispered as she ran her fingers over his bare chest, marveling at the slight changes in his appearance now that he'd become a god. His skin reminded her of the marble statues she'd thought he'd looked like when she first saw him. His eyes were even more vibrant in color as they bore into hers.

"Who needs luck when they have the Goddess of Destiny by their side?" Alexander asked as his lips came down, claiming hers. His hands ran down along her spine, resting on her round ass as he pulled her in closer to him.

Moerae moaned softly as she pressed her body more firmly against his—her happiness complete.

~*~*~

Alexander groaned and picked Moerae up. She wrapped her legs and arms around him as he carried her back into the room and threw her down on the bed. He took a moment to admire the way she looked with her hair sprawled out over the bed. Her golden eyes glowing with desire. He thought back to the first time they were together, when she tied him up and tormented him; he decided it was his turn to torment her. "Roll over," Alexander commanded in a deep voice.

Moerae stared the glint in his eyes while excitement filled her face and she did as he commanded.

Alexander undid his belt and instead of dropping it to the floor, he draped it around his neck, then finished removing his dress slacks and knelt on the bed next to her. He took the belt from around his neck and swung it lightly, bringing it down on her ass cheeks. He heard the sharp intake of her breath, then brought his hand down to rub her where the belt had hit. He couldn't help himself as he let his fingers brush against her clit to feel the wetness between her thighs and felt himself instantly grow even harder. "You're so damn wet. You like being spanked, don't you?"

"Yes," Moerae admitted as her cheeks flushed slightly.

Pulling his hand away, he swung the belt again, striking each of her lush ass cheeks...once, twice before rubbing them with his hand and this time, dipping his fingers deeper inside her.

Using his other hand, he swung the belt, spanking her ass cheeks some more as his fingers continued to stroke her slick folds, causing her to moan.

"Please, I need you." Moerae pleaded.

Alexander removed his fingers from within her, using both hands he wrapped the belt around her wrists and tightened it…restraining her. Then, he positioned himself between her legs and pulled up on her hips slightly, raising her ass into the air as he plunged into her quick and hard.

~*~*~

Moerae couldn't believe it when the belt struck her ass cheek. She thought it would hurt but instead, it only inflamed her passion. With each strike, she kept getting wetter and wetter and then his fingers were stroking her until she wasn't able to bear it any longer, she had to have him inside her.

Then, as if he knew she'd reached the edge of desperation, he was pounding into her, fast and hard. She could feel his balls slapping against her pussy, adding to the sensations going through her body. She wanted to reach out and grasp something—anything, but her hands were bound tightly with his belt. It should have infuriated, her instead she found her senses heightened.

Moerae couldn't take much more and when Alexander reached around her body, his fingers finding the bud of her clit—that was all it took. Throwing back her head, she cried out as her body convulsed with her climax, but he didn't stop there, he kept pounding into her and rubbing her, causing aftershocks from her orgasms to course through her body.

Just when she thought her body couldn't possibly handle any more, her new husband spilled into her, causing her to cry out in yet another orgasm.

Moerae collapsed, unable to move while she felt Alexander undo the binding around her wrist, allowing her arms to drop down limply on the bed. "I love you, Alexander," Moerae whispered, unable to muster the strength to even turn towards him.

He brushed kisses up along her spine, working his way towards her throat. "I love you too, Moerae."

His breath fanned out over her sensitive skin causing goose bumps to cover her flesh.

"And I will spend the rest of my life thanking the gods for allowing the twist in our destinies, so we could be together forever."

Moerae mustered the strength to turn, so she could face him. "Forever," she whispered back, happy that she wasn't going to be alone anymore. From now on, she was going to be living life, not just writing it for others and feeling alone. This was the happiest she'd ever felt in all of her long existence. She brought her lips to his and ran her fingers through his hair, holding him close to her

LEIGH SAVAGE

Leigh Savage lives in Saint Louis, MO with her husband and two children. Leigh is known for her paranormal erotic romance novels Angel of Death and Shadows of My Past.

"I grew up loving to escape in the world of stories that my Father would write just for me. So, it wasn't any wonder that as I got older, I too picked up the pen and started writing."

Follow Me On...

Facebook Fan Page:

http://www.facebook.com/groups/leighsavage/

Facebook: http://www.facebook.com/AuthorLeighSavage

Amazon: **amazon.com/author/leighsavage**

GoodReads: http://www.goodreads.com/leighsavage